THE SNOW GOOSE

The Snow Goose

By

PAUL GALLICO

Illustrations by
PETER SCOTT

MICHAEL JOSEPH

First published in Great Britain by Michael Joseph Limited
27 Wrights Lane, Kensington, London W8
November 1941
Forty-fourth impression December 1977
This illustrated edition first published December 1946
Twenty-fourth impression July 1986

ISBN 0 7181 0426 9

Printed in Great Britain by
Hollen Street Press Ltd, Slough, Berkshire
and bound by Dorstel Press, Harlow, Essex

I

THE GREAT MARSH LIES ON THE ESSEX COAST BETWEEN the village of Chelmbury and the ancient Saxon oyster-fishing hamlet of Wickaeldroth. It is one of the last of the wild places of England, a low, far-reaching expanse of grass and reeds and half-submerged meadowlands ending in the great saltings and mud flats and tidal pools near the restless sea.

Tidal creeks and estuaries and the crooked, meandering arms of many little rivers whose mouths lap at the edge of the ocean cut through the sodden land that seems to rise and fall and breathe with the recurrence of the daily tides. It is desolate, utterly lonely, and made lonelier by the calls and cries of the wildfowl that make their homes in the marshlands and saltings—the wildgeese and the gulls, the teal and widgeon, the redshanks and curlews that pick their way through the tidal pools. Of human habitants there are none, and none are seen, with the occasional exception of a wild-fowler or native oyster-fishermen, who still ply a trade already ancient when the Normans came to Hastings.

Greys and blues and soft greens are the colours, for when the skies are dark in the long winters, the many waters of the beaches and marshes reflect the cold and sombre colour. But sometimes, with sunrise and sunset, sky and land are aflame with red and golden fire.

Hard by one of the winding arms of the little River Aelder runs the embankment of an old sea wall, smooth

and solid, without a break, a bulwark to the land against the encroaching sea. Deep into a salting some three miles from the North Sea it runs, and there turns north. At that corner its face is gouged, broken, and shattered. It has been breached, and at the breach the hungry sea had already entered and taken for its own the land, the wall, and all that stood there.

At low water the blackened and ruptured stones of the ruins of an abandoned lighthouse show above the surface, with here and there, like buoy markers the top of a sagging fence-post. Once this lighthouse abutted on the sea and was a beacon on the Essex coast. Time shifted land and water, and its usefulness came to an end.

Lately it served again as a human habitation. In it there lived a lonely man. His body was warped, but his heart was filled with love for wild and hunted things. He was ugly to look upon, but he created great beauty. It is about him, and a child who came to know him and see beyond the grotesque form that housed him to what lay within, that this story is told.

It is not a story that falls easily and smoothly into sequence. It has been garnered from many sources and from many people. Some of it comes in the form of fragments from men who looked upon strange and violent scenes. For the sea has claimed its own and spreads its rippled blanket over the site, and the great white bird with the black-tipped pinions that saw it all from the beginning to the end has returned to the dark, frozen silences of the northlands whence it came.

2

IN THE LATE SPRING OF 1930 PHILIP RHAYADER CAME TO the abandoned lighthouse at the mouth of the Aelder. He bought the light and many acres of marshland and salting surrounding it.

He lived and worked there alone the year round. He was a painter of birds and of nature, who, for reasons, had withdrawn from all human society. Some of the reasons were apparent on his fortnightly visits to the little village of Chelmbury for supplies, where the natives looked askance at his mis-shapen body and dark visage. For he was a hunchback and his left arm was crippled, thin and bent at the wrist, like the claw of a bird.

They soon became used to his queer figure, small but powerful, the massive, dark, bearded head set just slightly below the mysterious mound on his back, the glowing eyes and the clawed hand, and marked him off as "that queer painter chap that lives down to lighthouse."

Physical deformity often breeds hatred of humanity in men. Rhayader did not hate; he loved very greatly, man, the animal kingdom, and all nature. His heart was filled with pity and understanding. He had mastered his handicap, but he could not master the rebuffs he suffered, due to his appearance. The thing that drove him into seclusion was his failure to find anywhere a return of the warmth that flowed from him. He repelled women. Men would have warmed to him had they got to know him. But the mere fact that an effort was being made hurt Rhayader and drove him to avoid the person making it.

He was twenty-seven when he came to the Great Marsh. He had travelled much and fought valiantly before he made the decision to withdraw from a world in which he could not take part as other men. For all the artist's sensitivity and woman's tenderness locked in his barrel breast, he was very much a man.

In his retreat he had his birds, his painting, and his boat. He owned a sixteen-footer, which he sailed with wonderful skill. Alone, with no eyes to watch him, he managed well with his deformed hand, and he often used his strong teeth to handle the sheets of his billowing sails in a tricky blow.

He would sail the tidal creek and estuaries and out to sea, and would be gone for days at a time, looking for new species of birds to photograph or sketch, and he became an adept at netting them to add to his collection

of tamed wildfowl in the pen near his studio that formed the nucleus of a sanctuary.

He never shot over a bird, and wild-fowlers were not welcome near his premises. He was a friend to all things wild, and the wild things repaid him with their friendship.

Tamed in his enclosures were the geese that came winging down the coast from Iceland and Spitsbergen each October, in great skeins that darkened the sky and filled the air with the rushing noise of their passage—the brown-bodied pink-feet, white-breasted barnacles, with their dark necks and clowns' masks, the wild white fronts with black-barred breasts, and many species of wild ducks —widgeon, mallard, pintails, teal, and shovellers.

Some were pinioned, so that they would remain there as a sign and signal to the wild ones that came down at each winter's beginning that here were food and sanctuary.

Many hundreds came and remained with him all through the cold weather from October to the early spring, when they migrated north again to their breeding-grounds below the ice rim.

Rhayader was content in the knowledge that when storms blew, or it was bitter cold and food was scarce, or the big punt guns of the distant bag hunters roared, his birds were safe; that he had gathered to the sanctuary and security of his own arms and heart these many wild and beautiful creatures who knew and trusted him.

They would answer the call of the north in the spring, but in the fall they would come back, barking and whooping and honking in the autumn sky, to circle the landmark of the old light and drop to earth near by to be his guests again—birds that he well remembered and recognized from the previous year.

And this made Rhayader happy, because he knew that implanted somewhere in their beings was the germ knowledge of his existence and his safe haven, that this knowledge had become a part of them and, with the coming of the grey skies and the winds from the north, would send then unerringly back to him.

For the rest, his heart and soul went into the painting of the country in which he lived and its creatures. There are not many Rhayaders extant. He hoarded them jealously, piling them up in his lighthouse and the store-rooms above by the hundreds. He was not satisfied with them, because as an artist he was uncompromising.

But the few that have reached the market are master-pieces, filled with the glow and colours of marsh-reflected light, the feel of flight, the push of birds breasting a morning wind bending the tall flag reeds. He painted the loneliness and the smell of the salt-laden cold, the eternity and agelessness of marshes, the wild, living creatures, dawn flights, and frightened things taking to the air, and winged shadows at night hiding from the moon.

3

ONE NOVEMBER AFTERNOON, THREE YEARS AFTER RHAYADER
had come to the Great Marsh, a child approached the
lighthouse studio by means of the sea wall. In her arms
she carried a burden.

She was no more than twelve, slender, dirty, nervous
and timid as a bird, but beneath the grime as eerily
beautiful as a marsh faery. She was pure Saxon, large-
boned, fair, with a head to which her body was yet to
grow, and deep-set, violet-coloured eyes.

She was desperately frightened of the ugly man she had
come to see, for legend had already begun to gather about
Rhayader, and the native fowl-hunters hated him for
interfering with their sport.

But greater than her fear was the need of that which
she bore. For locked in her child's heart was the knowledge, picked up somewhere in the swampland, that this

ogre who lived in the lighthouse had magic that could heal injured things.

She had never seen Rhayader before and was close to fleeing in panic at the dark apparition that appeared at the studio door, drawn by her footsteps—the black head and beard, the sinister hump, and the crooked claw.

She stood there staring, poised like a disturbed marsh bird for instant flight.

But his voice was deep and kind when he spoke to her.

"What is it, child?"

She stood her ground, and then edged timidly forward. The thing she carried in her arms was a large white bird, and it was quite still. There were stains of blood on its whiteness and on her kirtle where she had held it to her.

The girl placed it in his arms. "I found it, sir. It's hurted. Is it still alive?"

"Yes. Yes, I think so. Come in, child, come in."

Rhayader went inside, bearing the bird, which he placed

upon a table, where it moved feebly. Curiosity overcame fear. The girl followed and found herself in a room warmed by a coal fire, shining with many coloured pictures that covered the walls, and full of a strange but pleasant smell.

The bird fluttered. With his good hand Rhayader spread one of its immense white pinions. The end was beautifully tipped with black.

Rhayader looked and marvelled, and said: "Child, where did you find it?"

"In t' marsh, sir, where fowlers had been. What—what is it, sir?"

"It's a snow goose from Canada. But how in all heaven came it here?"

The name seemed to mean nothing to the little girl. Her deep violet eyes, shining out of the dirt on her thin face, were fixed with concern on the injured bird.

She said: "Can 'ee heal it, sir?"

"Yes, yes," said Rhayader. "We will try. Come, you shall help me."

There were scissors and bandages and splints on a shelf, and he was marvellously deft, even with the crooked claw that managed to hold things.

He said: "Ah, she has been shot, poor thing. Her leg is broken, and the wing tip, but not badly. See, we will clip her primaries, so that we can bandage it, but in the spring the feathers will grow and she will be able to fly again. We'll bandage it close to her body, so that she cannot move it until it has set, and then make a splint for the poor leg."

Her fears forgotten, the child watched, fascinated, as he worked, and all the more so because while he fixed a fine splint to the shattered leg he told her the most wonderful story.

The bird was a young one, no more than a year old. She was born in a northern land far, far across the sea, a land belonging to England. Flying to the south to escape the snow and ice and bitter cold, a great storm had seized her and whirled and buffeted her about. It was a truly terrible storm, stronger than her great wings, stronger than anything. For days and nights it held her in its grip and there was nothing she could do but fly before it. When finally it had blown itself out and her sure instincts took her south again, she was over a different land and surrounded by strange birds that she had never seen before. At last, exhausted by her ordeal, she had sunk to rest in a friendly green marsh, only to be met by the blast from the hunter's gun.

"A bitter reception for a visiting princess," concluded Rhayader. "We will call her the Lost Princess. And in a few days she will be feeling much better. See!" He reached into his pocket and produced a handful of grain. The snow goose opened its round brown eyes and nibbled at it.

The child laughed with delight, and then suddenly caught her breath with alarm as the full import of where she was pressed in upon her, and without a word she turned and fled out of the door.

"Wait, wait!" cried Rhayader, and went to the entrance, where he stopped so that it framed his dark bulk. The girl

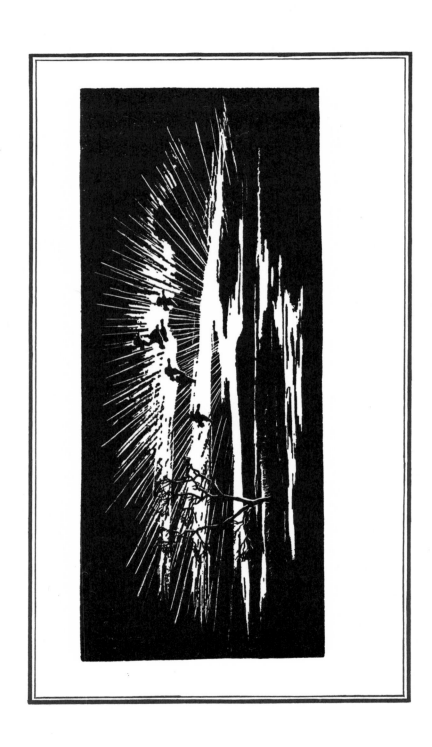

was already fleeing down the sea wall, but she paused at his voice and looked back.

"What is your name, child?"

"Frith."

"Eh?" said Rhayader. "Fritha, I suppose. Where do you live?"

"Wi' t' fisherfolk at Wickaeldroth." She gave the name the old Saxon pronunciation.

"Will you come back to-morrow, or the next day, to see how the Princess is getting along?"

She paused, and again Rhayader must have thought of the wild water birds caught motionless in that split second of alarm before they took to flight.

But her thin voice came back to him: "Ay!"

And then she was gone, with her fair hair streaming out behind her.

The snow goose mended rapidly and by midwinter was already limping about the enclosure with the wild pink-footed geese with which it associated, rather than the barnacles, and had learned to come to be fed at Rhayader's call. And the child, Fritha, or Frith, was a frequent visitor. She had overcome her fear of Rhayader. Her imagination was captured by the presence of this strange white princess from a land far over the sea, a land that was all pink, as she knew from the map that Rhayader showed her, and on which they traced the stormy path of the lost bird from its home in Canada to the Great Marsh of Essex.

Then one June morning a group of late pink-feet, fat and well fed from the winter at the lighthouse, answered the stronger call of the breeding-grounds and rose lazily, climbing into the sky in ever widening circles. With them, her white body and black-tipped pinions shining in the spring sun, was the snow goose. It so happened that Frith was at the lighthouse. Her cry brought Rhayader running from the studio.

"Look! Look! The Princess! Be she going away?"

Rhayader stared into the sky at the climbing specks.

"Ay," he said, unconsciously dropping into her manner of speech. "The Princess is going home. Listen! she is bidding us farewell."

Out of the clear sky came the mournful barking of the pink-feet, and above it the higher, clearer note of the snow goose. The specks drifted northward, formed into a tiny V, diminished, and vanished.

With the departure of the snow goose ended the visits of Frith to the lighthouse. Rhayader learned all over again the meaning of the word "loneliness."

That summer, out of his memory, he painted a picture of a slender, grime-covered child, her fair hair blown by a November storm, who bore in her arms a wounded white bird.

4

IN MID-OCTOBER THE MIRACLE OCCURRED, RHAYADER WAS in his enclosure, feeding his birds. A grey north-east wind was blowing and the land was sighing beneath the incoming tide. Above the sea and the wind noises he heard a clear, high note. He turned his eyes upward to the evening sky in time to see first an infinite speck, then a black-and-white pinioned dream that circled the lighthouse once, and finally a reality that dropped to earth in the pen and came waddling forward importantly to be fed, as though she had never been away. It was the snow goose. There was no mistaking her. Tears of joy came to Rhayader's eyes. Where had she been? Surely not home to Canada. No she must have summered in Greenland or Spitzbergen with the pink-feet. She had remembered and had returned.

When next Rhayader went into Chelmbury for supplies, he left a message with the postmistress—one that must have caused her much bewilderment. He said: "Tell Frith, who lives with the fisherfolk at Wickaeldroth, that the Lost Princess has returned."

Three days later, Frith, taller, still tousled and unkempt, came shyly to the lighthouse to visit the snow goose.

Time passed. On the Great Marsh it was marked by the height of the tides, the slow march of the seasons, the passage of the birds, and, for Rhayader, by the arrival and departure of the snow goose.

The world outside boiled and seethed and rumbled with the eruption that was soon to break forth and come close to marking its destruction. But not yet did it touch upon Rhayader, or, for that matter, Frith. They had fallen into a curious natural rhythm, even as the child grew bolder. When the snow goose was at the lighthouse, then she came, too, to visit and learn many things from Rhayader.

They sailed together in his speedy boat, that he handled so skilfully. They caught wildfowl for the ever-increasing colony, and built new pens and enclosures for them. From him she learned the lore of every wild bird, from gull to gyrfalcon, that flew the marshes. She cooked for him sometimes, and even learned to mix his paints.

But when the snow goose returned to its summer home, it was as though some kind of bar was up between them, and she did not come to the lighthouse. One year the bird did not return, and Rhayader was heartbroken. All things seemed to have ended for him. He painted furiously through the winter and the next summer, and never once saw the child. But in the fall the familiar cry once more rang from the sky, and the huge white bird, now at its full growth, dropped from the skies as mysteriously as it had departed. Joyously, Rhayader sailed his boat into Chelmbury and left his message with the postmistress.

Curiously, it was more than a month after he had left the message that Frith reappeared at the lighthouse, and

Rhayader, with a shock, realized that she was a child no longer.

After the year in which the bird had remained away, its periods of absence grew shorter and shorter. It had grown so tame that it followed Rhayader about and even came into the studio while he was working.

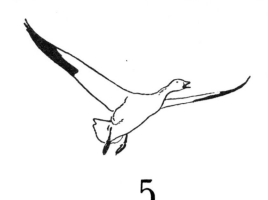

5

the Great Marsh. The world was on fire. The whine and roar of the bombers and the thudding explosions frightened them. The first day of May, Frith and Rhayader stood shoulder to shoulder on the sea wall and watched the last of the unpinioned pink-feet and barnacle geese rise from their sanctuary; she, tall, slender, free as air and hauntingly beautiful; he, dark, grotesque, his massive bearded head raised to the sky, his glowing dark eyes watching the geese form their flight tracery.

"Look, Philip," Frith said.

Rhayader followed her eyes. The snow goose had taken flight, her giant wings spread, but she was flying low, and once came quite close to them, so that for a moment the spreading black-tipped, white pinions seemed to caress them and they felt the rush of the bird's swift passage.

Once, twice, she circled the lighthouse, then dropped to earth again in the enclosure with the pinioned geese and commenced to feed.

"She be'ent going," said Frith, with marvel in her voice. The bird in its close passage seemed to have woven a kind of magic about her. "The Princess be goin' t' stay."

"Ay," said Rhayader, and his voice was shaken too. "She'll stay. She will never go away again. The Lost Princess is lost no more. This is her home now—of her own free will."

The spell the bird had girt about her was broken, and Frith was suddenly conscious of the fact that she was frightened, and the things that frightened her were in Rhayader's eyes—the longing and the loneliness and the deep, welling, unspoken things that lay in and behind them as he turned them upon her.

His last words were repeating themselves in her head as though he had said them again: "This is her home now —of her own free will." The delicate tendrils of her instincts reached to him and carried to her the message of the things he could not speak because of what he felt himself to be, mis-shapen and grotesque. And where his voice might have soothed her, her fright grew greater at his silence and the power of the unspoken things between them. The woman in her bade her take flight from something that she was not yet capable of understanding.

Frith said: "I—I must go. Good-bye. I be glad the—the Princess will stay. You'll not be so alone now."

She turned and walked swiftly away, and his sadly spoken "Good-bye, Frith," was only a half-hearted ghost of a sound borne to her ears above the rustling of the marsh grass. She was far away before she dared turn for a backward glance. He was still standing on the sea wall, a dark speck against the sky.

Her fear had stilled now. It had been replaced by something else, a queer sense of loss that made her stand quite still for a moment, so sharp was it. Then, more slowly, she continued on, away from the skyward-pointing finger of the lighthouse and the man beneath it.

6

returned to the lighthouse. May was at its end, and the
day, too, in a long golden twilight that was giving way to
the silver of the moon already hanging in the eastern sky.

She told herself, as her steps took her thither, that she
must know whether the snow goose had really stayed, as
Rhayader said it would. Perhaps it had flown away, after
all. But her firm tread on the sea wall was full of eagerness,
and sometimes unconsciously she found herself hurrying.

Frith saw the yellow light of Rhayader's lantern down
by his little wharf, and she found him there. His sailboat
was rocking gently on a flooding tide and he was loading
supplies into her—water and food and bottles of brandy.
When he turned to the sound of her coming, she saw that
he was pale, but that his dark eyes, usually so kind and

placid, were glowing with excitement, and he was breathing heavily from his exertions.

Sudden alarm seized Frith. The snow goose was forgotten. "Philip! Ye be goin' away?"

Rhayader paused in his work to greet her, and there was something in his face, a glow and a look, that she had never seen there before.

"Frith! I am glad you came. Yes, I must go away. A little trip. I will come back." His usually kind voice was hoarse with what was suppressed inside him.

Frith asked: "Where must ye go?"

Words came tumbling from Rhayader now. He must go to Dunkirk. A hundred miles across the sea. A British army was trapped there on the sands, awaiting destruction at the hands of the advancing Germans. The port was in flames, the position hopeless. He had heard it in the village when he had gone for supplies. Men were putting out from Chelmbury in answer to the government's call, every tug and fishing boat or power launch

that could propel itself was heading across the North Sea to haul the men off the beaches to the transports and destroyers that could not reach the shallows, to rescue as many as possible from the Germans' fire.

Frith listened and felt her heart dying within her. He was saying that he would sail the open sea in his little boat. It could take six men at a time; in a pinch, seven. He could make many trips from the beaches to the transports.

The girl was young, primitive, inarticulate. She did not understand war, or what had happened in France, or the meaning of the trapped army, but the blood within her told her that here was danger.

"Philip! Must 'ee go? You'll not come back. Why must it be 'ee?"

The fever seemed to have gone from Rhayader's soul with the first rush of words, and he explained it to her in terms that she could understand.

He said: "Men are huddled on the beaches like hunted birds, Frith, like the wounded and hunted birds we used to find and bring to sanctuary. Over them fly the steel peregrines, hawks, and gyrfalcons, and they have no shelter from these iron birds of prey. They are lost and storm-driven and harried, like the snow goose you found and brought to me out of the marshes many years ago, and we healed her. They need help, my dear, as our wild creatures have needed help, and that is why I must go. It is something that I can do. Yes, I can. For once—for once I can be a man and play my part."

Frith stared at Rhayader. He had changed so. For the first time she saw that he was no longer ugly or mis-shapen or grotesque, but very beautiful. Things were turmoiling in her own soul, crying to be said, and she did not know how to say them.

"I'll come with 'ee, Philip."

Rhayader shook his head. "Your place in the boat would cause a soldier to be left behind, and another, and another. I must go alone."

He donned rubber coat and boots and took to his boat. He waved and called back: "Good-bye! Will you look after the birds until I return, Frith?"

Frith's hand came up, but only half, to wave too. "God speed you," she said, but gave it the Saxon turn. "I will take care of t' birds. God-speed, Philip."

It was night now, bright with moon fragment and stars and northern glow. Frith stood on the sea wall and watched the sail gliding down the swollen estuary. Suddenly from the darkness behind her there came a rush of wings, and something swept past her into the air. In the night light she saw the flash of white wings, black-tipped, and the thrust-forward head of the snow goose.

It rose and cruised over the lighthouse once and then headed down the winding creek where Rhayader's sail was slanting in the gaining breeze, and flew above him in slow, wide circles.

White sail and white bird were visible for a long time.

"Watch o'er him. Watch o'er him," Frith whispered. When they were both out of sight at last, she turned and walked slowly, with bent head, back to the empty light-house.

7

NOW THE STORY BECOMES FRAGMENTARY, AND ONE OF
these fragments is in the words of the men on leave who
told it in the public room of the Crown and Arrow, an
East Chapel pub.

"A goose, a blooming goose, so 'elp me," said Private
Potton, of His Majesty's London Rifles.

"Garn," said a bandy-legged artilleryman.

"A goose it was. Jock, 'ere, seed it same as me. It come
flyin' down outa the muck an' stink an' smoke of Dunkirk
that was over'ead. It was white, wiv black on its wings,
an' it circles us like a bloomin' dive bomber. Jock, 'ere,
'e sez: 'We're done for. It's the hangel of death a-come
for us.'

" 'Garn,' Hi sez, 'it's a ruddy goose, come over from 'ome wiv a message from Churchill, an' 'ow are we henjoying the bloomin' bathing. It's a omen, that's what it is, a bloody omen. We'll get out of this yet, me lad.'

"We was roostin' on the beach between Dunkirk an' Lapanny, like a lot o' bloomin' pigeons on Victoria Hembankment, waitin' for Jerry to pot us. 'E potted us good too. 'E was be'ind us an' flankin' us an' above us. 'E give us shrapnel and 'e give us H.E., an' 'e peppers us from the bloomin' hatmosphere with Jittersmiths.

"An' offshore is the *Kentish Maid*, a ruddy hexcursion scow wot Hi've taken many a trip on out to Margate in the summer, for two-and-six, waiting to take us off, 'arf a mile out from the bloomin' shallows.

"While we are lyin' there on the beach, done in an' cursin' becos there ain't no way to get out to the boat, a Stuka dives on 'er, an' 'is bombs drop alongside of 'er, throwin' up water like the bloomin' fountains in the palace gardens; a reg'lar display it was.

D

"Then a destroyer come up an' says: 'No, ye don't' to the Stuka with ack-acks and pom-poms, but another Jerry dives on the destroyer, an' 'its 'er. Coo, did she go up! She burned before she sunk, an' the smoke a' the stink come driftin' inshore, all yellow, an' black, a' out of it comes this bloomin' goose, a-circlin' around us trapped on the beach.

"An' then around a bend 'e comes in a bloody little sailboat, sailing along as cool as you please, like a bloomin' toff out for a pleasure spin on a Sunday hafternoon at 'Enley."

" 'Oo comes?" inquired a civilian.

" 'Im! 'Im that saved a lot of us. 'E sailed clean through a boil of machine-gun bullets from a Jerry in a Jittersmith wot was strafin'—a Ramsgate motorboat wot 'ad tried to take us off 'ad been sunk there 'arf an hour ago—the water was all frothin' with shell splashes an' bullets, but 'e didn't give it no mind, 'e didn't. 'E didn't 'ave no petrol to burn or hexplode, an' he sailed in between the shells.

"Into the shallows 'e come out of the black smoke of the burnin' destroyer, a little dark man wiv a beard, a bloomin' claw for a 'and, an' a 'ump on 'is back.

"'E 'ad a rope in 'is teeth that was shinin' white out of 'is black beard, 'is good 'and on the tiller an' the crooked one beckonin' to us to come. An' over'ead, around and around, flies the ruddy goose.

"Joc, 'ere, says: 'Lawk, it's all over now. It's the bloody devil come for us 'imself. Hi must 'ave been struck an' don't know it.'

"'Garn,' I sez, 'it's more like the good Lord, 'e looks to me, than any bloomin' devil.' 'E did, too, like the pictures from the Sunday-school books, wiv 'is white face and dark eyes an' beard an' all, and 'is blooming boat.

"'Hi can take seven at a time,' 'e sings out when 'e's in close.

"Our horfficer shouts: 'Good, man! . . . You seven nearest, get in.'

"We waded out to where 'e was. Hi was that weary Hi

couldn't climb over the side, but 'e takes me by the collar of me tunic an' pulls, wiv a 'In ye go, lad. Come on. Next man.'

"An' in Hi went. Coo, 'e was strong, 'e was. Then 'e sets 'is sail, part of wot looks like a bloomin' sieve from machine-gun bullets, shouts: 'Keep down in the bottom of the boat, boys, in case we meet any of yer friends,' and we're off, 'im sittin' in the stern wiv 'is rope in 'is teeth, another in 'is crooked claw, an' 'is right 'and on the tiller, a-steerin' an' sailin' through the spray of the shells thrown by a land battery somewhere back of the coast. An' the bloomin' goose is flyin' around and around, 'onking above the wind and the row Jerry was makin', like a bloomin' Morris on Winchester by-pass.

" 'Hi told you yon goose was a omen,' Hi sez to Jock. 'Look at 'im there, a bloomin' hangel of mercy.'

" 'Im at the tiller just looks up at the goose, wiv the rope in 'is teeth, an' grins at 'er like 'e knows 'er a lifetime.

" 'E brung us out to the *Kentish Maid* and turns around

and goes back for another load. 'E made trips all afternoon an' all night too, because the bloody light of Dunkirk burning was bright enough to see by. Hi don't know 'ow many trips 'e made, but 'im an' a nobby Thames Yacht Club motorboat an' a big lifeboat from Poole that come along brought off all there was of us on that particular stretch of hell, without the loss of a man.

"We sailed when the last man was off, an' there was more than seven hunder' of us haboard a boat built to take two hunder'. 'E was still there when we left, an' 'e waved us good-bye and sails off towards Dunkirk, and the bird wiv 'im. Blimy, it was queer to see that ruddy big goose flyin' around 'is boat, lit up by the fires like a white hangel against the smoke.

"A Stuka 'ad another go at us, 'arfway across, but 'e'd been stayin' up late nights, an' missed. By mornin' we was safe 'ome.

"Hi never did find out what become of 'im, or 'oo 'e was—'im wiv the 'ump an' 'is little sail-boat. A bloody good man 'e was, that chap."

"Coo," said the artilleryman. "A ruddy big goose. Whatcher know?"

8

IN AN OFFICER'S CLUB IN BROOK STREET, A RETIRED NAVAL officer, sixty-five years old, Commander Keith Brill-Oudener, was telling of his experiences during the evacuation of Dunkirk. Called out of bed at four o'clock in the morning, he had captained a lopsided Limehouse tug across the Straits of Dover, towing a string of Thames barges, which he brought back four times loaded with soldiers. On his last trip he came in with her funnel shot away and a hole in her side. But he got her back to Dover.

A naval-reserve officer, who had two Brixham trawlers and a Yarmouth drifter blasted out from under him in the last four days of the evacuation, said: "Did you run across that queer sort of legend about a wild goose? It was all up and down the beaches. You know how those things spring up. Some of the men I brought back were talking about it. It was supposed to have appeared at intervals the last days between Dunkirk and La Panne. If you saw it, you were eventually saved. That sort of thing."

"H'm'm'm," said Brill-Oudener, "a wild goose. I saw a tame one. Dashed strange experience. Tragic in a way, too. And lucky for us. Tell you about it. Third trip back. Toward six o'clock we sighted a derelict small boat. Seemed to be a cap or a body in her. And a bird perched on the rail.

"We changed our course when we got nearer, and went over for a look-see. By Gad, it was a chap. Or had been, poor fellow. Machine-gunned, you know. Badly. Face down in the water. Bird was a goose, a tame one.

"We drifted close, but when one of our chaps reached over, the bird hissed at him and struck at him with her wings. Couldn't drive it off. Suddenly young Kettering, who was with me, gave a hail and pointed to starboard. Big mine floating by. One of Jerry's beauties. If we'd kept on our course we'd have piled right into it. Ugh! Head on. We let it get a hundred yards astern of the last barge, and the men blew it up with rifle-fire.

"When we turned our attention to the derelict again, she was gone. Sunk. Concussion, you know. Chap with her. He must have been lashed to her. The bird had got up and was circling. Three times, like a plane saluting. Dashed queer feeling. Then she flew off to the west. Lucky thing for us we went over to have a look, eh? Odd that you should mention a goose."

9

the Great Marsh, taking care of the pinioned birds, waiting
for she knew not what. The first days she haunted the sea
wall, watching; though she knew it was useless. Later she
roamed through the storerooms of the lighthouse building
with their stacks of canvases on which Rhayader had
captured every mood and light of the desolate country
and the wondrous, graceful, feathered things that inha-
bited it.

Among them she found the picture that Rhayader had
painted of her from memory so many years ago, when she
was still a child, and had stood, wind-blown and timid,
at his threshold, hugging an injured bird to her.

The picture and the things she saw in it stirred her as
nothing ever had before, for much of Rhayader's soul
had gone into it. Strangely, it was the only time he had

painted the snow goose, the lost wild creature, storm-driven from another land, that to each had brought a friend, and which, in the end, returned to her with the message that she would never see him again.

Long before the snow goose had come dropping out of a crimsoned eastern sky to circle the lighthouse in a last farewell, Fritha, from the ancient powers of the blood that was in her, knew that Rhayader would not return.

And so, when one sunset she heard the high-pitched, well-remembered note cried from the heavens, it brought no instant of false hope to her heart. This moment, it seemed, she had lived before man times.

She came running to the sea wall and turned her eyes, not toward the distant sea whence a sail might come, but to the sky from whose flaming arches plummeted the snow goose. Then the sight, the sound, and the solitude surrounding broke the dam within her and released the surging, overwhelming truth of her love, let it well forth in tears.

Wild spirit called to wild spirit, and she seemed to be flying with the great bird, soaring with it in the evening sky, and hearkening to Rhayader's message.

Sky and earth were trembling with it and filled her beyond the bearing of it. "Frith! Fritha! Frith, my love. Good-bye, my love." The white pinions, black-tipped, were beating it out upon her heart, and her heart was answering: "Philip, I love 'ee."

For a moment Frith thought the snow goose was going to land in the old enclosure, as the pinioned geese set up a welcoming gabble. But it only skimmed low, then soared up again, flew in a wide, graceful spiral once around the old light, and then began to climb.

Watching it, Frith saw no longer the snow goose but the soul of Rhayader taking farewell of her before departing for ever.

She was no longer flying with it, but earth-bound. She stretched her arms up into the sky and stood on tip-toes, reaching, and cried: "God-speed! God-speed, Philip!"

Frith's tears were stilled. She stood watching silently long after the goose had vanished. Then she went into the lighthouse and secured the picture that Rhayader had painted of her. Hugging it to her breast, she wended her way homeward along the old sea wall.

I O

EACH NIGHT, FOR MANY WEEKS THEREAFTER, FRITH CAME to the lighthouse and fed the pinioned birds. Then one early morning a German pilot on a dawn raid mistook the old abandoned light for an active military objective, dived on to it, a screaming steel hawk, and blew it and all it contained into oblivion.

That evening, when Fritha came, the sea had moved in through the breached walls and covered it over. Nothing was left to break the utter desolation. No marsh fowl had dared to return. Only the frightless gulls wheeled and soared and mewed their plaint over the place where it had been.